ABOUT THIS BOOK

TWO QUEENS OF HEAVEN:
APHRODITE • DEMETER
Doris Gates

Aphrodite, goddess of love and jealousy, was the most beautiful and feared of the Olympian goddesses. She worked her magic on the hearts of men and women and was indifferent to the tragic outcome of her meddling. Demeter, the Good Goddess, oversaw the harvest and brought fruitfulness to the earth. "Her suffering and generous bounty made her the most revered of all the queens of heaven."

Here also are the stories of:

Persephone—daughter of Demeter and doomed to be the wife of the God of the Underworld

Adonis—beloved of Aphrodite

Pygmalion—sculptor of the beautiful statue which came to life

Eros—son of Aphrodite

Leander—who swam the furious Hellespont for his love, Hero

Pyramus and Thisbe—the lovers to whom Aphrodite brought tragedy

TWO · QUEENS · OF · HEAVEN ·

APHRODITE
°°°
DEMETER

Doris Gates

Illustrated by Trina Schart Hyman

Puffin Books

Penguin Books Ltd, Harmondsworth, Middlesex, England
Penguin Books, 40 West 23rd Street, New York, New York 10010, U.S.A.
Penguin Books Australia Ltd, Ringwood, Victoria, Australia
Penguin Books Canada Limited, 2801 John Street, Markham, Ontario, Canada L3R 1B4
Penguin Books (N.Z.) Ltd, 182–190 Wairau Road, Auckland 10, New Zealand

First published by The Viking Press 1974
Published in Puffin Books 1983
Copyright © 1974 by Doris Gates
All rights reserved

Library of Congress Cataloging in Publication Data
Gates, Doris, date. Two queens of heaven.
(The Greek myths series)
Summary: Retells the Greek myths in which Aphrodite,
goddess of love and beauty, and Demeter, goddess of
grain and agriculture, play major roles.
1. Aphrodite—Juvenile literature. 2. Demeter
(Greek deity)—Juvenile literature. [1. Aphrodite
(Greek deity) 2. Demeter (Greek deity) 3. Mythology,
Greek] I. Hyman, Trina Schart, ill. II. Title. III. Series.
BL820.V5G37 1983 292 83-8136 ISBN 0-14-031646-9

Printed in the United States of America by
Offset Paperback Mfrs., Dallas, Pennsylvania

Contents

*These stories are all dedicated
to the boys and girls of
Fresno County, California,
who heard them first*

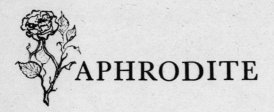

APHRODITE

FROM · THE · SEA · FOAM

1

THE SUN SHONE BRIGHT on the blue water. A little breeze ruffled its surface. Zephyr, god of the west wind, was on hand to celebrate a great occasion. A new goddess was about to be added to the family of gods on Mount Olympus, one who would make men and gods know the ecstasy of love and the satisfactions of beauty. She would be called Aphrodite, Aphrodite of the sweet smiles. Poets would sing of her beauty, and the Graces themselves would serve as her handmaidens. Gods and men alike would be helpless before her charms. She would be a queen of heaven.

Not far off the coast of Cythera, there appeared a gathering of foam on the water. It resembled the white spindrift that trails behind a great wave as it breaks. But this foam did not trail. It formed itself into a raft rising and falling with the sea. Suddenly a woman's figure appeared atop the raft, balancing on slender feet. She was young, and beautiful beyond anything in human form the sun had ever shone on. Her lips, sweetly curved, were smiling. Her sparkling eyes gazed confidently upon the waters at her feet. And her hair, garlanded with roses and flowing golden about her, partially cloaked her graceful figure.

Gently Zephyr blew the foam-born creature to the island, where she stepped ashore. Grass and flowers sprang up under her feet, a pattern of fragrance and color for Aphrodite, goddess of love and beauty.

As she bent to wring the sea water from her long hair, Aphrodite was joined by the three Graces—Aglaia, Euphrosyne, and Thalia. These daughters of Zeus, ruler of Olympus, embodied the essence of gaiety, laughter, festival, and song. They were always together, sometimes dancing to Apollo's lyre. Now here they were to attend upon Aphrodite and accompany her to high Olympus, home of the gods. Arraying her splendidly, they assisted her into a conch shell which had appeared at the water's edge. With Zephyr blowing steadily and the Graces circling gaily upon the water around it, the conch shell with its enchanting passenger was blown eastward across the water to the island of Cyprus. There Aphrodite and her three attendants were welcomed by an entourage sent from Zeus to escort this great goddess to Olympus.

So Aphrodite came to join the family of gods. Zeus married her to Hephaestus, god of the forge. They subsequently became the parents of a daughter, Harmonia, who became the wife of Cadmus, founder of Thebes.

THE·STORY·OF·ADONIS

2

AS THE GODDESS OF LOVE, Aphrodite often worked upon the hearts of men and women. Her meddling usually brought woe to her victims. Aphrodite was ruthlessly indifferent to the tragic outcome of her meddlings. Nor did she worry about her husband's feelings when she took Ares, god of war, as a lover.

She had love affairs with many mortals, too. One of these was a youth named Adonis. Aphrodite loved Adonis from the moment he was born. Since his birth was under a cloud, she took it upon herself to protect this babe. She put him in a chest and carried the chest to Persephone, wife of Hades, god of the Underworld.

But Persephone, lonely in her dark, cavernous kingdom, took the infant Adonis into her arms and refused to give him up when Aphrodite later claimed him as her own.

Zeus at last was forced to take a hand in their jealous quarrel. He decreed that Adonis should spend one third of the year with Persephone and one third with Aphrodite. The remaining third the youth could have as his own. When he was grown to manhood, Adonis, flattered by the love of the beautiful Aphrodite, chose to spend his free time with her, too.

Aphrodite became obsessed by her love for this exceedingly handsome young man. She abandoned Hephaestus, Ares, and all her other loves to follow after Adonis, who was by now an enthusiastic hunter. She quite forsook Olympus and, hoisting her skirts about her, sped through forest and over meadow in pursuit of Adonis. Not even Artemis, goddess of the hunt, was more devoted to the chase than the goddess of love and beauty.

One day when the two were resting from the hunt, Aphrodite said to Adonis:

"Dear lad, it seems to me that you grow bolder in the hunt as the years go by. Today you took a dreadful chance when you cornered that huge boar against the cliff. Had he not managed to escape, not even your dogs could have saved you, for your spear was in him. Think of me and the grief I would suffer if you were lost to me."

Adonis smiled. "Do not be afraid for me, dear love," he told her. "Your being here, close to me, is proof that the gods are on my side. What harm could come to any man beloved of Aphrodite?"

A slight pucker marred her smooth brow. She understood the nature of the gods as this mortal never could. And some, like Ares, might seek revenge for her fickle behavior.

"There is much in what you say," she replied to Adonis. "And yet I warn you to be careful. Seek the smaller animals. Avoid the stout and fearless lion and boar."

But Adonis, taking her into his arms, withheld his promise.

Shortly thereafter, Aphrodite summoned her two white swans and yoked them to her chariot. Then, taking tender leave of her lover, she rode up into the sky, the swans' wide wings bearing the chariot aloft.

She had not yet flown out of sight when Adonis called his dogs to him and, plunging into the thick of the woods, sought to find the trail of the wounded boar he had lost. It did not take the dogs long. An excited baying told the young hunter they had found their quarry. Coming at last to where the bedlam of their howls and yappings smote the rocky cliff, Adonis saw his boar at bay. The spear, caught in the animal's tough hide, trailed at its side. The beast was weakened by loss of blood, but the maddening pain of the weapon had charged him with more than usual strength and courage. As Adonis moved to seize his spear, the boar rushed recklessly at the dog pack, which parted before him. In the next instant he was on the young hunter and, knocking him flat, sank his tusks into his enemy's groin. Adonis let out a terrible groan as the blood spilled from his body. He tried to rise, but fell back, mortally wounded.

High in her swan-drawn chariot, Aphrodite heard that groan and knew it for what it was. Wheeling the birds about, she returned to the glade where she had taken farewell of her lover. She left the chariot and followed his trail into the woods, guided by the bellowings of his dog pack. Soon she came upon Adonis lying on the blood-wet ground.

"Oh, my dear love," she cried. "What awful woe is this!"

She dropped beside him and tried to lift his body in her arms, seeing at once that it was too late to save him. She managed at last to get his drooping head against her breast and rained tears and kisses upon his lifeless face.

When her grief had spent itself, Aphrodite gently laid the body of Adonis on the ground and stood above it, mourning.

"Your death must never be forgotten, Adonis. Each year on this day, Earth shall mourn for you, and in token of this grief, a flower shall spring from your blood."

As she spoke, Aphrodite took from her bodice a small vial and poured some of its contents on the still body at her feet. Instantly the bloodied earth began to bubble as a spring bubbles up, moving the grains of sand in its clear depths. In less than an hour, a flower grew from the bubbling—a red flower, red as blood: the anemone.

It is said that the boar had been sent by Artemis in disgust over Aphrodite's infatuation with the mortal Adonis. It is also said that the boar was jealous Ares in disguise. Whichever is true, the goddess of love never ceased to mourn her dead Adonis. The anemone is a symbol of her grief.

ANCHISES·AND·APHRODITE

3

IT IS AN UNPLEASANT FACT of human nature that many families have a trouble-maker born into them. For the family on Mount Olympus, Aphrodite filled this role. Not only did she cause dissension with her love affairs, but she criticized and mocked those gods who had sired children with a mortal. Though she too had loved a mortal, Adonis, she had not borne him a child, she smugly reminded them.

Naturally the gods resented such taunting, and very soon Olympus was in an uproar. At last, Zeus, weary of the wrangling, decided to take a hand in it. He would stop Aphrodite's taunts in such a way that she would never indulge in them again.

Now at this time Anchises, son of the king of Dardania, was guarding his father's flocks on the slopes of

Mount Ida near the city of Troy. He was an unusually handsome young man, strong and alert. It was this unfortunate young prince whom Zeus chose as his instrument for punishing Aphrodite.

One day as the goddess was riding in her swan-drawn chariot, she happened to glide above the spot where Anchises watched over his sheep. Zeus, who was closely watching Aphrodite's every move, caused her to look down from her chariot. At the same instant, Eros sent an arrow into her heart. These arrows, shot into the heart of god or mortal, instantly cause the victim to fall in love with the first person met of the opposite sex. So, as she noted the young shepherd below her, Aphrodite fell madly in love with him. Never had she felt such passion for anyone, not even for Adonis.

She immediately began a descent to earth, but before the swans had quite reached the gentle slope, a sudden insight warned her. If she appeared suddenly as a goddess before the youth, he would be greatly startled and might even flee from her. It was well known among mankind that no good could come from romantic dealings with the gods.

So Aphrodite climbed the sky again, away from Mount Ida. Her mind was busy with a plan of seduction as she flew south to Cyprus. There she summoned her handmaidens, the Graces, and had herself adorned in such garments as a woman of royalty might wear. She even removed the girdle that was a symbol of her power and that made her irresistible to gods and men alike.

"I am beautiful enough without it," she observed, as she studied herself in the mirror the Graces held up to her. "Whoever that youth may be, he will not be able to withstand the power of my beauty along with the power of my love. But I must not let him know I am a goddess, and the girdle would give me away."

Back in her chariot, Aphrodite drove her swans north to Mount Ida. So impatient was the goddess to arrive there that though the air around the chariot whistled from the speed of the great white wings, still she urged the swans to quicken their flight.

In remarkably short time, Aphrodite saw the green slopes of Mount Ida below her. She guided the chariot to a grove of trees at a distance from where she had first seen Anchises. Gently the chariot touched the ground, and the goddess descended from it. She carefully resettled her blown garments and smoothed her hair. Then, wearing the sweet smile for which she was famous, she started walking through the grove.

She had hardly taken a dozen steps when trotting from among the trees came all manner of wild animals. Bears, lions, tigers, wolves. They fawned upon her, their hearts filled with desire. Such was the power of the goddess of love.

Aphrodite scattered them with an imperious gesture.

"Be gone," she commanded them. "I'll attend to your wants later. Leave me in peace now to gratify my own."

Zeus, watching from Olympus, smiled.

Anchises had erected a tent to one side of the meadow

where his flock grazed. Here—it being midday—he had
settled himself to rest. As Aphrodite emerged from the
grove, she looked carefully around her. No one was in
sight, but she saw the tent across the meadow. Surmising
that the object of her search was within, she started toward it.

Anchises had taken up his lyre and was about to strike
it when Aphrodite's shadow fell across the entrance to
the tent.

Like most young men, Anchises had often speculated
casually as to what his first love would be like. He had
not yet seen the woman he wished to marry. But now as he
looked up, alerted by the shadow, he was quite sure she
stood before him. The lyre fell from his hands. Never
had he imagined such loveliness. He rose slowly from the
couch, stunned by the sudden vision.

"Who are you?" he whispered.

"My father is king of Phrygia," lied Aphrodite. "And
you?"

"Anchises," he replied, "and equally royal. But tell
me, beautiful stranger, how do you happen to be here in
this rude spot?"

Aphrodite entered the tent and gracefully sank upon
the couch like one weary and spent.

"It is a long tale," she said. "Enough that Hermes
brought me here against my will to be your bride." She
dropped her gaze and blushed becomingly. Anchises was
enchanted. "The gods seem to have willed it," she mur-
mured.

"You said you came here against your will. Would it still be against your will if you knew I loved you? For I do," declared Anchises.

Aphrodite shook her head. "Now that I behold your goodness and manliness I am not loath to accept the gods' decision."

At her words, the smitten youth swept her off the couch and into his arms. For a moment the goddess allowed herself to enjoy his caresses. Then she drew away.

"Dear Anchises, now take me to your father and mother and send ambassadors to Phrygia that my own parents may know my happy fate. Let all be done properly in preparation for our nuptials."

All was done as she wished, and Aphrodite became the bride of Anchises. In time, she bore him a son whom she named Aeneas. Zeus's plan had worked perfectly; never again would Aphrodite be able to taunt the gods for their half-mortal offspring.

Aphrodite's loves were not enduring, and she soon became bored with her mortal lover. Before the birth of their son, Aphrodite revealed her true identity to Anchises. Anchises was shocked and frightened at the revelation. He knew no good could come to him from this marriage with a goddess. Nor did it.

Following her confession, Aphrodite warned Anchises never to disclose their union to anyone. She wished to keep her child's divine heritage a secret from all the world. Anchises was to say Aeneas was the child of a nymph.

The secret gnawed at Anchises as secrets have a way of doing. At last he could not resist boasting of his love affair with a queen of heaven, Aphrodite, and of the son she had borne to him.

As usual, his boastings were soon known on Mount Olympus. Not only Aphrodite, but Zeus was furious that a tattling mortal should have brought humiliation upon one of the gods. To punish him, Zeus hurled a thunderbolt at Anchises. It hit him on the leg, crippling him for life.

Years later, Aeneas became a stout warrior fighting on the side of Troy in the long war between the Greeks and the Trojans. Dardania was an ally of Troy.

When the city fell, Aeneas fled the burning ruins carrying the aged and crippled Anchises on his shoulders. They escaped to Sicily where Anchises died and was buried.

Aeneas, son of Aphrodite, became the founder of Rome and was the hero of one of the greatest epics of the Western world—the *Aeneid* by the Latin poet, Virgil.

PYGMALION

4

ON THE ISLAND OF CYPRUS, sacred to Aphrodite, there lived a sculptor named Pygmalion. The man was a fine artist and his studio was a gathering place for his admirers. They marveled at the way he worked in stone and ivory, fashioning figures that seemed so real a visitor would sometimes put out a hand and touch the statue to make sure it was not living flesh.

Now Pygmalion hated women; no one knew exactly why. Some said he had been disappointed in love; others that he had had a cruel mother who had resented his birth. In any case, Pygmalion lived alone in his studio, and no woman ever came there. Nor had he ever fashioned a statue in the form of a woman.

But one day Pygmalion was seized with a great desire to sculpt a woman. He was shocked and bewildered by the sudden urge.

"Has mischievous Aphrodite put this spell upon me?" he asked himself. "And, if so, to what purpose?"

He tried to ignore the strange desire, but in vain. It kept him from sleep. It hounded his every waking moment. At last he gave in to it.

As he reluctantly started work upon the statue, he felt ashamed of what he was doing. He banished all visitors from his studio. No one must ever learn of his self-betrayal. Nor would they, for of course when the sculpture was completed and the strange urge satisfied, he would destroy it.

As the statue began to take form under his hands, a compelling interest in it seized Pygmalion. At first he had thought to fashion an ugly female figure, completely without grace and with a face so ugly no man would look upon it without loathing. If this were Aphrodite's trick, it should not succeed whatever her intent.

But as he began to cut away the marble to the point where the figure began to emerge from the rude block, Pygmalion's hands seemed to act on their own. Day after day the figure grew and began to take on beauty. Despite his best intentions, Pygmalion was fashioning an object so ravishing that even he began to feel a grudging admiration for it. The chiseled face wore an expression so soft and beguiling it was hard to imagine it was only stone. The sculptor, gazing on it in amazement, smiled as he had never before smiled upon a woman. But, of course, this was merely a statue!

Then came the final polishing of the marble. Pygmalion smoothed it until it glowed, even taking on the lucent, ivory tone of healthy young flesh. His hands moved almost lovingly upon it.

At last the day came when nothing remained to be done. The life-sized statue stood upon its pedestal complete and utterly lovely. Pygmalion walked slowly around it, and when he came to where its face looked sweetly down upon him, a violent passion gripped him. He fell in love!

Now began a period of perfect misery for Pygmalion. The pangs of unrequited love are torment, especially when the object of that love is there before the sufferer day and night. Pygmalion tried to embrace the lovely figure, but the cold stone repulsed him. For all its fleshly appearance, it was stone, unfeeling and unyielding.

"Ah, if you could but speak to me," Pygmalion exclaimed to the face bending above him. "Your eyes look into mine, your lips smile, almost opening to speak, yet you are ever silent."

He remembered his intention to destroy the statue, but that was unthinkable now. Life would lose all meaning without this lovely creation. Then in his desperation and frustration, Pygmalion began to fantasize about his marble love. He saw her as really human. He talked to her. He robed her in silken garments. He even tucked her into bed at night with a pillow beneath her head. He brought her gifts young girls prize—flowers, birds, and

pretty stones. The bare and cluttered studio became a kind of bower for his beloved, while his sculptor's tools gathered dust.

Then came the day that was sacred to Aphrodite on the island of Cyprus. Altars everywhere were decked with roses, her favorite flower. Snow-white heifers, garlanded and with their horns tipped with gold, were led to the sacrifice by lads and maidens in their rarest finery. All the people were celebrating, Pygmalion among them.

Half-fearfully, he approached an altar where incense sent up its sweet fragrance. There he offered a prayer to the great goddess.

"Oh, Aphrodite, protector of lovers, listen to me now. If it be in your power, then send me a wife like the woman I have sculpted. Until now I have shunned the company of women, detesting them above all creatures. But now I acknowledge my fault in this and any affront it may have offered to you, great goddess of love and beauty. Only grant me such a wife as I crave, and I will honor you above all Immortals."

It so happened that Aphrodite, invisible, was present at that altar to hear Pygmalion's prayer. Perhaps she had indeed induced him to carve that statue. If so, then she must have watched with amusement his infatuation with it. It would not have pleased the goddess of love that any man should spurn her sex. Whatever her reasons, Aphrodite now listened to Pygmalion's prayer and was moved by its sincerity. Still, she did not disclose her presence, and Pygmalion left the altar wondering with little hope if his prayer would be answered.

Straight home he went to torment himself with gazing on his beloved statue. But as he approached the pedestal where each day he placed her, he stopped amazed. Were his eyes playing him tricks, or had he simply gone mad? She was smiling at him as before, only there was a difference in the smile. It was wider, warmer, and her eyes had a sparkle that no marble could produce. As he gazed, a warm color rose into her cheeks. He rushed forward and seized her hand. It was warm within his own and he could feel a pulse beating faintly under his thumb. The statue was alive!

With a glad cry, Pygmalion lifted his arms, and the statue stepped lightly down and into them.

Pygmalion gave his love the name, Galatea. Soon their marriage was celebrated. They became the parents of a son called Paphos for whom an island was later named. And as far as anyone knows, they lived happily ever after.

5

The Calydonian Hunt

THE TROUBLE ALL STARTED when Oeneus, king of Calydon forgot to do honor to Artemis. Thankful for a good harvest, the king had made offerings to Demeter, who received the first of the harvested grain. Dionysus, god of wine, was offered the first crushing of the grapes, which were plentiful that year. Athena, as her due, was given a richly painted amphora of olive oil from the tree sacred to her. Only Artemis was overlooked. This was unfortunate since she was a vengeful goddess.

To punish King Oeneus for his insulting oversight, Artemis sent a dreadful boar to ravage his kingdom. It was huge beyond any of its breed that men had seen before. Its tusks curved white and sharp as scimitars on each side of its heavy jaws, and its eyes shone red with constant rage. This dreadful monster roared about the countryside, tearing down the grapevines, uprooting trees, trampling the grain. It even attacked the cattle grazing in the fields, and neither men nor dogs could prevail against it.

At last the king sent out a call for help. He invited all the heroes of Greece to hasten to his country where a challenge in the shape of this monstrous boar awaited them. The heroes were not slow to respond because they welcomed this chance to show their courage and skill.

Among these heroes were Theseus, conqueror of the terrible Minotaur; the famous sons of Leda—Castor and Pollux; Meleager, son of Oeneus; and a mighty hunter, Peleus, who would become the father of famed Achilles; and many others. Not even Jason, who led the Argonauts in search of the Golden Fleece, could boast a greater company.

The last to answer the summons of King Oeneus, and the most surprising, was a maiden huntress named Atalanta. She was lovely to look upon as she stood confidently among the young men, an ivory quiver hanging from her left shoulder. Her hair was bound back in a close-held knot, revealing a face at once boyish and feminine. A polished buckle held her robe at the neck, and in her right hand she carried a bow.

Atalanta's story was well known and her ability as a hunter widely respected.

She had been born in Arcadia. Her father, who had set his heart on a son, was so disappointed in this small daughter that he gave orders for the babe to be exposed on a mountain side, there to die of hunger. Luckily a she-bear discovered the newborn child and gave her nourishment. And so, among animals and kindly hunters, Atalanta grew to maidenhood, a wild creature of the woods. Somehow she and her father rediscovered each other and became reconciled. But Atalanta never abandoned her hunter's life. She roamed the woods and fields with a spirit free and fearless. Like other such maidens before her, she vowed never to marry.

The king's son, Meleager, was not slow to notice Atalanta's charms.

"Happy the man who wins her for his bride," he told himself.

He had little time for romantic speculation however. A dangerous task lay before them, and all were eager to get started on it.

The hounds were rounded up, and the nets for capturing the quarry were carefully checked. Then the band of heroes set out to hunt the Calydonian boar.

They knew the boar was resting from his most recent forays in a virgin wood that rose on the opposite side of the plain that spread itself below the palace of King Oeneus. The hunters crossed the plain and climbed to where the forest loomed above it, dark and threatening. Here they spread their nets among the trees, then loosed the dogs.

Hardly had the hounds taken the trail when the boar came crashing through the underbrush straight at the hunters. His sudden appearance created havoc among them at first, and two men were downed before any could hurl their spears. Some, aiming too quickly, threw their weapons only to have them fall wide of their mark as the huge creature rushed upon them, slashing to right and left with his sharp tusks. One man, Nestor, who was to win fame in the Trojan War, escaped death by using his spear to vault into a tree. From that safe vantage point, he watched the battle raging below him.

At length, Atalanta fixed an arrow to her bow and, taking careful aim, let it fly. It struck the boar under one ear, drawing blood. Quickly the creature's bristles were stained a vivid red.

Meleager had witnessed Atalanta's shot, and now he let out a glad cry, proud of her marksmanship. She at least had managed to wound the boar while none of the others had struck a weapon into him.

But his comrades were ashamed that a woman had accomplished what they had failed to do. Goaded by their humiliation, the heroes became reckless as they rushed to a fresh attack. Though wounded, the boar was still full of fight, and another man paid with his life for his daring.

Theseus begged the companion who had accompanied him to take care.

"Brave men can fight at a distance," Theseus warned him.

From a distance he hurled his own bronze-tipped

spear. But a tree branch deflected it, and the spear struck one of the dogs.

Now Meleager strode forward, a spear in each hand. The first one missed, but the second struck the animal's broad back. The beast whirled with rage and pain.

Without hesitating a moment, Meleager picked up his spent weapon and, striding up to the wounded boar, drove the spear straight through its shoulder to the heart. The boar crashed to the ground, dead.

Meleager's Fate

WITH GLAD SHOUTS, the men ran forward to shake the victor's hand and to dip their spears in the boar's blood. Meleager, as a victory gesture, placed a foot on the boar's head and addressed his companions.

"The prize belongs to the maid from Arcadia," he told them. "She it was who first wounded the boar and made my victory possible. To her must go the head and skin."

He drew his hunting knife and began severing the great head with its gleaming tusks. Next he ripped off a section of skin from the broad back. While he was thus engaged, a murmuring began among the heroes. They resented a woman's taking these trophies. What right had she to the spoils? She had not killed the boar. But for Meleager's plain lovesickness, there would be no possibility of her having them.

"Come Atalanta," Meleager called to her when at last he had finished with the carcass. "Come and receive your just reward for valor and marksmanship."

Atalanta stepped forward and took the bloody prize into her hands. But hardly had they closed upon it when two uncles of Meleager's, his mother's brothers, strode up and snatched it away from her.

"Don't depend too much upon your beauty, woman," one of them cried to her. "Not all of us are lovesick like my nephew here. You have no right to the prize. If Meleager is so sick-hearted as to waive his rights to it, then we shall draw lots among us for the boar's head and tusks and hide. Nor shall you take part in that drawing."

At these insulting words, Meleager's wrath leaped up like a flame among dry leaves. Without a moment's hesitation he plunged his hunting knife, bright with the boar's blood, into the heart of the speaker. The man's brother thought to avenge him, but fear of Meleager held him back. Then Meleager sprang toward the second of his uncles, the knife still dripping with his kinsman's blood, and ran him through. The others stood stunned before the swift and dreadful deeds. And dreadful would be Meleager's punishment for the killings.

At the time of his birth, the three Fates had visited Meleager's mother, whose name was Althaea. They had informed her that this infant son would live only so long as the log burning on the hearth should last. Althaea instantly sprang from the birth-bed and, seizing the burn-

ing brand in her naked hand, beat out its flame, and hid the darkened remains in a stout chest far at the back of a secret cupboard. There it had lain all the years Meleager was growing up, known only to Althaea.

Now on this fateful day Althaea was at the altar of Artemis, praying to the goddess that her son would be spared from the boar's attack. As she knelt there, the sounds of mourning were suddenly borne to her ears. Was Meleager already dead? She ran from the temple to discover the bodies of her two brothers being carried into the city. Grieving, she bent above them. But when she learned of how they had died, her grief changed to rage. Two good men and true were dead and at her son's own hand! She would have her revenge upon him for this crime. Under such circumstances, a sister's grief would outweigh a mother's love. Althaea hastened to the palace.

Straight to the secret cupboard she went and drew forth the chest. The blackened log still lay within. She gathered shavings and placed them on the hearth and lighted them. Then she started to lay the brand upon the flame. Her hand drew back. Again she forced it forward and again drew back. Twice more she hesitated. Then she flung the brand on the flame and stood before the fire stony-faced until the log was consumed.

At the moment the brand began to burn, Meleager, striding toward the city, was stricken with terrible pain. His weapons fell from his hands, and he crumpled to the ground. As the minutes passed, he grew weaker and weaker. By the time the brand had become ashes, he lay dead. The prophecy of the Fates had been fulfilled.

There was great mourning throughout all Calydon for the loss of this prince. But Althaea suffered most. At last her remorse became so great she could not live with it, and she hanged herself.

Thus did Artemis take her revenge upon King Oeneus for his insult to her. And though it ended in victory for the heroes, men would long remember the tragic outcome of the Calydonian boar hunt.

Atalanta's Race

MEANWHILE ATALANTA, none the worse for her Calydonian experience, had returned to her Arcadian haunts. But news of her great beauty had spread as a result of that gathering of heroes, and suitors began flocking to her father's house. They became such a nuisance that at last the bedeviled man begged his daughter to give consideration to his plight.

"It is useless to suppose that you can forever withstand Aphrodite's powers. Nor can I longer turn a deaf ear to the pleading of these worthy men. You must choose among them."

She answered her father, "I shall never choose among

them. But if they wish to compete for my hand, I will accommodate them. Let them all line up and race against me. Whichever one of them wins the race will win my hand. But if I outrun them, then their lives will be forfeit."

Atalanta was as famous for swiftness of foot as for beauty. No man had ever outdistanced her in the hunt or in a footrace.

It was a cruel offer, but so great was her beauty the suitors were willing to chance it.

Naturally, news of the contest quickly spread throughout all Greece, and one young man, Hippomenes, journeyed from afar to witness it. He was curious to see men foolish enough to risk their lives for a mere woman.

He sat apart and watched as one by one the suitors took their places at the starting line.

Then Atalanta appeared.

For a startled instant Hippomenes supposed a goddess had come among them. And then he saw the girl take her place with the men. This, then, was the famed Atalanta! Hippomenes marveled that a mortal could claim such perfection.

"It is I who am the fool," he told himself. "What man wouldn't risk his life for such a woman? And I must have my chance at her, too. May none of these win over her that my opportunity to race with her may come," he prayed.

The signal was given, and the race began. Atalanta sprang forward. As if sandaled by Hermes, her bare feet skimmed the ground. Her short tunic blew back against her body so that all its lovely outlines were exposed. And her hair, loose now, floated straight behind her white shoulders. Never had mortal woman appeared so beautiful.

It was soon apparent to Hippomenes that his prayer would be answered. Atalanta sped in front of her pursuers almost at once. By the time the last lap was run, she was an easy victor. The losers groaned, remembering the fate that awaited them.

Now it was Hippomenes' turn.

He rose and went to meet Atalanta as she came off the field.

"Atalanta," he addressed her, "why race against men who are plainly not in condition for any athletic contest? They are slow-footed and short-winded. I am neither. And I am nobly born. Poseidon, himself, sired my great-grandfather. Let us race, and if I win against you, you will not need to be ashamed of my blood."

As he spoke, Atalanta experienced a strange feeling. Should they race, she half-hoped that he might win. The thought frightened her, and she fought to smother it. Of course she would win! What sudden madness had hinted at any other outcome? She would win and he would die. Along with the knowledge faced so boldly, Atalanta suddenly, unaccountably, suffered an unaccustomed pang —regret that one so handsome and so young should have to die.

"Stranger," she said, "return safely to your home and

there seek the hand of any maid you choose. Surely none will refuse you. You saw the many I defeated and whose lives are forfeit. You must be tired of living that you should seek to race with Atalanta."

But Hippomenes stubbornly demanded his chance against the maiden, and at last her father and the on-lookers insisted that the stranger be allowed his race.

The pair walked slowly to the starting line. Atalanta was reluctant to race at all, while Hippomenes sought a few moments of time to send up a prayer to Aphrodite.

"Dear Cyprian," he whispered, "who has lighted this flame of love within my breast, now help me. Either quicken my feet or slow Atalanta's. No other altar will be as sacred to me as yours if only you will conspire to let me win this race."

Aphrodite heard his prayer and decided to help him.

On the island of Cyprus, in the center of a fertile field, there grew a most wondrous tree. Its leaves and branches were of purest gold, and it bore golden apples. Aphrodite happened to be passing the tree when she heard Hippomenes' prayer. Quickly she plucked three golden apples from a golden bough and rushed, invisible, to Hippomenes. She continued invisible to all but him as she handed over the three golden apples and told him what to do with them.

Again the signal was given, and the two runners darted forward as one. But instead of passing Hippomenes, Ata-lanta ran easily beside him the better to admire the athlete's manly beauty. But when the youth was about to draw ahead of her, Atalanta put on a sudden burst of speed and was about to pass him when he drew from his tunic one of the golden apples and tossed it in front of her. Atalanta broke stride, tempted by the bright object. She measured the distance between herself and Hippomenes and, deciding she had time, swooped and seized the apple, and Hippomenes darted ahead.

The crowd cheered wildly and urged him on. The cheers changed to groans when Atalanta came abreast of Hippomenes and again was about to pass him. Again a golden apple was rolled into her path, and again she slowed to get it. Hippomenes flew down the course, his speed gaining as his hopes rose. Twice now he had shown his heels to this girl, something no one had ever done before.

Now the spirit of contest flamed in Atalanta. She felt chagrined that her longing for the golden fruit had threatened her victory. No longer did she feel compassion for this youth. She would run as ruthlessly as she had ever done. Soon she was abreast of Hippomenes, and though the apples gathered in her tunic hampered her efforts, she was running in front of him when Hippomenes threw the last golden apple. He tossed it far to the edge of the course, where it rolled into the grass, a bright temptation. They were nearing the end of the course and Atalanta hesitated. Should she risk it with the end so near? Was it possible that this apple gleamed more

brightly than the other two? Temptation overcame her.
She sped from the course, seized the apple, and returned.
But Hippomenes was across the finish line. He had won
the race and a bride!

Hand in hand they left the field, Hippomenes waving
in triumph to the exulting crowd. Atalanta kept her
eyes upon the ground, but no sullen disappointment
looked out of her face. Instead, she wore a smile almost
as sweet as Aphrodite's own. She held the golden apples
cuddled in one arm, and an extraordinarily comely youth
strode at her side.

CUPID · AND · PSYCHE

6

A Fearsome Oracle

THIS STORY CONCERNS EROS, the god of love and son of
Aphrodite. Since it comes to us from Roman rather than
Greek mythology, he is called by the Latin name Cupid.

Many of the stories concerning Cupid, or Eros, picture
him as a young child, dimpled and pretty and armed
with a small bow and a quiver of golden arrows. However, the story of Cupid and Psyche shows the small god
grown to young manhood, and beautiful as only the son
of Aphrodite could be.

Psyche was the daughter of a king and had two sisters.
Her beauty was so great that all who beheld it forsook
Aphrodite and began worshiping Psyche instead. This
was a terrible affront to the goddess. But the girl, despite
her beauty, had no suitors. So awe-inspiring was her loveliness that all men, though admiring, were afraid of her

beauty. Both her sisters, much less favored, found worthy husbands. Psyche was left at home, worshiped and alone.

Aphrodite, when she discovered that her altars were abandoned while Psyche's were honored, was, of course, perfectly furious. She went at once to her young son and commanded that he make Psyche fall in love with some mortal who was repulsive in every way.

"Let it be some filthy goatherd," she commanded, "and may this odious maiden for the rest of her life tend the fire in his sooty hut. Let her go barefoot and ragged, the slave of her brutish husband. Her altars will be deserted then!"

Cupid hastened away to do his mother's bidding. But when he saw the beautiful maiden as she sat in the dappled sunlight of her father's garden, he fell madly in love with her. Cupid said nothing to his mother of his infatuation but, seeking Apollo, arranged a scheme with him by which he could secretly become Psyche's husband.

Hardly had the plan been decided on between the two gods, when the girl's father journeyed to Miletus, a city of Asia Minor noted for the oracle of Apollo residing there. The king offered the oracle rich gifts and then begged to know how his famous daughter could be freed from the dangerous worship of her beauty. He rightly feared Aphrodite's wrath.

The oracle's answer was a hard one. "Your daughter must go to the high mountaintop which lies near her home. There she must be abandoned by everyone, and there a monster will come and wed her. He is frightful beyond imagining, a terror even to the gods."

The father went home sorrowfully to tell the dreadful news to his daughter, for it never occurred to him to doubt the oracle, much less disobey it.

Psyche proved as brave as she was beautiful.

"Whatever fate the gods send me, I gladly accept," she said. "Let it be done at once as the oracle has directed." Then she went to array herself in her finest garments.

Later, attended by her sorrowing sisters and father and all the people of the city, Psyche was led to the mist-enshrouded mountain. Once safe upon its summit, she was then abandoned to await the coming of the monster. She peered intently into the swirling mists about her, fearful of what she would see, while her ears were alerted to the slightest sound. But, for a long time, she saw and heard nothing and marveled at the awful cruelty of this monster who would so wickedly prolong her agony.

The Castle in the Wood

SUDDENLY SHE FELT a light breeze, and at the same moment she was lifted gently off her feet and carried away from the mountain to a sunny meadow, where she was put safely down. All about her was sunlight and flowers and the sound of bird song. Astonished but still fearful, she looked about her. At a little distance she saw a wood, and rising above the trees, the turrets of a fine castle. Psyche started toward it.

The wood was not dark, but welcoming, with flowers growing between the trees where the sunlight filtered down. She climbed the wide shallow stairs to the terrace of the castle and approached its fine entrance. But before she could sound the knocker, the door swung wide, and voices from invisible presences bade her enter and be at home. She wandered at will through splendid rooms where music issued from the walls, though no musicians were anywhere in sight. And always above the music were the friendly, reassuring voices urging her not to be afraid but to consider herself the mistress of this place.

"Then this must be the home of the monster whose wife I now am," thought Psyche. "Surely he cannot mean me harm, for the voices are friendly."

She came at last to the banquet hall where a fine feast was spread. Somewhat reassured by this time, Psyche realized that she was hungry and sat down and ate heartily. Then, weary from all that she had experienced, she sought her bed, and the voices guided her to a richly furnished bower.

Some time during the night Psyche wakened suddenly. Someone was in the room; she could sense a presence. Was the monster, her husband, here at last? There was no light within the room, not even moonlight shining across the casement. And while she lay fearful and expectant, she felt a gentle hand brush back the hair from her brow, and a gentle voice whispered words of love into her ear. If this was a monster, he was like none she had ever heard of! She longed for daylight so that she might behold this mysterious husband who spoke so lovingly to her.

But when dawn came over the casement and Psyche rose expectantly from her pillow, no husband did she see. Again she was quite alone.

The Sisters' Visit

NOW THE DAYS SPED happily for Psyche. The castle and its grounds were hers to enjoy, while invisible servants fulfilled her every wish. And each night her husband came to her and each dawn vanished. She had yet to lay eyes on him.

But as usually happens when one's every wish is fulfilled, Psyche began to be bored. Besides, she was lonely. She longed to see her sisters. Perhaps she wanted them to know that the dreadful fate ordered for her had not been fulfilled, thus relieving their hearts of sorrow and anxiety. Perhaps, too, she longed to have them know the amazing luxury she now enjoyed, riches beyond any of their dreams.

One night she spoke of her longing to her husband.

"Dear one," he said, "can you not be content as we are? How will it add to your happiness to have your sisters come here? I swear their visit will only bring us distress, for they will envy you what you have since it is so much more than they can boast of."

But Psyche begged, and at last her husband gave in. "Very well," he said in a voice full of sorrow. "I will have Zephyr waft them here for a day's visit. But I warn you, do not let them talk you into trying to find out who I am. Only great misfortune will come to you if ever you try to look upon me."

Psyche promised, and the next day her sisters came.

Like any proud bride showing off her new home for the first time, Psyche conducted her sisters through the castle. They had greeted her with great affection and relief, but now as they surveyed the splendor in which she lived, they forgot the joy they had felt in discovering her safe and began to resent the good fortune she had found. Now she not only had her beauty but everything else her heart could desire. Who was Psyche that the gods should favor her so? Then, as the day advanced without sight of her husband who was providing all this splendor, another thought entered their envious minds. He must be a monster, after all, since their sister had failed to disclose his presence in the castle. Even though he had spared her life and lavished all manner of luxury upon her, he must be someone of whom she was ashamed. They began to ask her questions. What did her new husband look like? Why had they not yet met him?

Psyche put them off, explaining that he had gone on a hunt into a neighboring province and would not return for several days. But what did he look like? they insisted.

"Like any other man," said Psyche airily, "comely in his way but not overhandsome."

The sisters had to be satisfied with this report. When the day ended, Psyche filled their arms with gifts, and Zephyr wafted them back to the mountaintop.

When a few more days had passed, Psyche again wanted to see her sisters. Her husband remonstrated with her to no avail. Psyche was lonely; Psyche was bored; Psyche insisted. Reluctantly, her husband gave permission for the sisters' return, warning her once more of the danger.

When they appeared next morning, the sisters were ready for Psyche. They had come determined to find out about this mysterious husband of hers. When they demanded to know where he was and what he was like, Psyche, forgetting what she had already told them, gave different answers, and the sisters' suspicions were confirmed.

"You can be sure he is a real monster," said one.

"He is doubtless a serpent who is only biding his time until he will devour you without warning."

Psyche looked troubled and confused. Nothing in anything her husband had said or done had led her to believe he was evil. Yet her sisters' certainties stirred fears in her own mind. Perhaps he *was* only biding his time before he killed her.

"You must take a lamp and a knife," the eldest now told her, "and go to his bed while he is asleep and there kill him before he can waken. Only this can save you."

By the time they had departed at the end of the day, Psyche's mind was made up. This very night, she would gaze upon the being she had married.

After her husband had fallen asleep, Psyche slipped from her bed. Quietly she lighted a lamp and took up the knife she had put beside it. Then she approached the bed where her husband lay sleeping.

She dreaded knowing what she might see, and all her body tensed as she held the lamp high. Its gentle light revealed the figure of a young man asleep upon the couch. His lips, as sweetly curved as Aphrodite's, were slightly parted. Golden lashes curled from his closed eyelids, and his hair clung tight about his head in golden clusters. Psyche stood enraptured, and a long and thankful sigh escaped her. She lifted the lamp higher and saw long wings closed against the youth's back. The lamp wavered as the shock of this discovery smote the girl. Cupid! Her husband, then, was the god of love himself! Marveling, she bent toward him, and as she did, a drop of hot tallow from the lamp fell on his naked shoulder. Instantly, Cupid awoke. He stared for a moment into Psyche's astonished eyes before he leaped from the couch and through the window and into the night. Presently, from somewhere in the wood, she heard the god's voice.

"Ah, Psyche," he mourned, "now you have wrecked

our happiness and brought great woe upon yourself. Why did you not heed my warnings? Farewell, dear Psyche."

And Psyche, hearing it, knew that once again she was alone.

Psyche's Trials

PSYCHE SOUGHT TO UNDO the mischief at the shrines of Hera and Demeter. At both their altars she prayed for the return of her love. But the goddesses were deaf to her entreaties. They knew that Cupid had betrayed his mother by marrying her enemy, and they feared Aphrodite's wrath.

Not knowing what else to do, Psyche started searching for her lost husband. He, meanwhile, sought his mother's mansion on high Olympus, there to have the burn upon his shoulder treated. Thus Aphrodite learned of his marriage with her mortal enemy, and she again vowed revenge against Psyche even as she upbraided her son for his disobedience. He had made a fool of himself by marrying beneath him, his mother told him. As for the girl, she was a bigger fool for being suspicious of her love. She richly deserved punishment.

One day Psyche's wanderings brought her to a temple of Aphrodite. The desperate girl decided to enter it and by her prayers seek mercy of her husband's mother. But Aphrodite had warned the servants of all her temples against helping Psyche. So now they fell upon her and beat her most shamefully. Some time later the goddess herself seized Psyche and imprisoned her in a small room, its center heaped with a large mound of seeds, a mixture of all the grains that grow.

"Sort these by midnight, or it will go hard with you," the goddess told her.

The task was hopeless. But as Psyche knelt before the pile wondering how to begin, suddenly she saw a thin dark line advancing toward her from under the door. Thousands of ants were marching to her rescue. Surely this was Cupid's work, Psyche told herself. Perhaps her husband still loved her. Perhaps they would yet be reunited. The ants fell upon the seed pile, and by midnight when the goddess came to check on Psyche, all the seeds had been sorted into small heaps about the room.

Psyche tried hard to hide her elation as the angry goddess gazed upon the finished task.

But Aphrodite was not finished with this mortal.

The next morning, the goddess ordered the girl to bring her an armful of golden fleece from some sheep grazing on a riverbank not far away. The sheep were dangerous; many a man had paid with his life for trying to approach them.

"Have the fleece here by nightfall," said Aphrodite, "or it will go hard with you."

Psyche set out and came to the river. At a little distance she could see the shining sheep grazing quietly. Yet she dared not go near them. How would she obtain the fleece?

It was then she heard a small voice almost at her feet. A reed growing on the riverbank was speaking to her.

"Do not try to approach the sheep now," it warned her. "The rising sun makes them vicious. Wait until midday when they will have grazed sufficiently. Then they lie down under the trees, and the murmuring of the river makes them drowsy. It is then you must go forth among the shrubs and bushes where they have grazed and remove from the branches the fleece that has been caught there when the sheep brushed through."

Psyche did just as the reed told her and by nightfall returned with her arms full of shining fleece.

Thwarted again in her attempts to destroy the girl, Aphrodite set her another task still more difficult.

She pointed to a mountain, blue in the distance, and said, "You are to bring to me a jar of water from the spring that gushes from the base of that mountain."

Psyche bravely set forth. But when she reached the mountain and came to the rock where the stream gushed forth, she discovered that it was guarded by several huge serpents. The snakes hissed at her most horribly, and Psyche, clutching the jar to her, realized the hopelessness of her task.

This time Zeus intervened to help her. Psyche, he de-

cided, had been punished enough. Suddenly his great eagle swooped down, took the jar and, safely passing the serpents—which would not touch a servant of Zeus— filled it at the spring and returned the jar to Psyche.

Despite Zeus, Aphrodite's wrath was still not appeased. Psyche must perform one more task, the most hopeless of all.

Handing the girl a small box, Aphrodite said, "Take this to Persephone and tell her to put some of her beauty in it. I have lost a bit of mine nursing my son whose injury you caused. Be careful that you do not open the box after she has given it back to you."

Poor Psyche! What was she to do now? Persephone was the wife of Hades and queen of the dreadful Underworld inhabited by the Dead. What mortal could ever reach that region? Would old Charon ferry her across the river Styx? And how could she escape Cerberus, the three-headed dog that guarded the entrance to Hades' realm? There was no hope for her now, and in her desperation Psyche climbed to the top of a high tower, determined to throw herself down from it and end her torment.

But when she had reached the top of the tower, it, too, spoke to her.

"Do not end your life," it said. "You have only to put two coins under your tongue in payment for a trip both ways on Charon's ferry As for the dog, Cerberus, throw him some barley bread soaked in honey-water when you enter the abode of the Dead and on leaving it."

The tower gave her further good advice and ended by repeating Aphrodite's warning. "Be sure you do not open the box after Persephone returns it to you."

Grateful for her life, Psyche did all that the tower had directed. Charon accepted her coin and ferried her across the shadowy waters of the river Styx. Cerberus ceased his vicious growling when she flung him half the barley bread. And when she entered the dismal throne room of Persephone, the queen readily took the box, disappeared briefly with it, then returned and handed it back to her visitor.

Now Psyche could return to the upper world. Again Cerberus was appeased, and old Charon dourly accepted her second coin.

When she had come again into the world of sunlight and growing things, Psyche felt a terrible urge to open the little box. She knew that her own beauty must by this time be sadly diminished by the trials she had undergone. If she took just a little of what Persephone had given, surely Aphrodite would never know.

She cautiously opened the box. But no sooner had she lifted its lid than a deep sleep fell upon her, and she sank to the ground like one dead.

At this point Cupid took a hand in Psyche's sufferings. He was cured now of his wound, but not of his love. Seeing his dear Psyche lying like one dead filled him with such remorse that he forgot whatever fear he had of his vengeful mother. He drew an arrow from his quiver and lightly touched the sleeping girl with it. She woke to find her husband smiling into her eyes.

Taking her hand, Cupid led her to Mount Olympus and there entreated Zeus to bless their marriage and to allow Psyche to join the family of the Immortals.

"She has suffered much for my sake," he told the All-father, "and I love her well."

Zeus, moved by the beauty of the girl before him, granted Cupid's wish. And so Aphrodite was forced to make her peace with Psyche and never plotted her any further woe.

HERO · AND · LEANDER

7

IN THE NORTHERN REACHES of the Aegean Sea there lies a famous strait called the Dardanelles. In ancient times it was known as the Hellespont. It connects the Aegean with the Sea of Marmara, which in its turn, leads to the Black Sea.

Two cities once rose on opposite shores of this strait. One, Sestos, was the home of Hero, a priestess of the temple of Aphrodite. A mile across the water in Abydos dwelt an athlete named Leander.

A festival was being celebrated in Sestos in honor of Aphrodite. Leander happened to attend the festival, and there he saw Hero as she served at the silver altar. This loveliest of maidens was all grace as she went about her sacred duties. The colored veils draping her young body from shoulders to sandals flowed about her like water.

Before he knew it, Leander was in love. When Hero turned from the altar and met his gaze upon her, she, too, felt sudden passion. It was as if Eros had shot an arrow into each of their hearts.

When the festival was over, Leander declared his love and begged Hero to name a trysting place.

"Dear Leander, our love is hopeless," Hero told him. "Have you forgotten that I am Aphrodite's own priestess, and that she is a jealous goddess? I would be doomed if I were to give my love to anyone but her."

"And yet you already have," Leander reminded her.

"But Aphrodite does not know it."

"Nor need she," said Leander. "We can meet at night in the tower which rises above the shore not far from the temple. From there, Abydos is no more than a mile away. It is no distance at all even without a wind to fill my sail."

Still Hero shook her head. "Even on the darkest night a boat would be noticed when you came to shore. Someone would be sure to investigate if you came often. And if we were discovered together, it could be death for us both."

Leander smiled. "Then I shall forgo the boat."

Hero looked inquiringly at him.

"I shall swim across. You will set a flaming torch outside the tower wall, and with that to guide me, I can do it safely."

What maiden could withstand such valor and determination? Certainly not Hero. Her love overcame her misgivings, and the tryst was agreed upon. Night after night, Hero placed the torch in its bracket on the sea wall. Then, hiding within the tower, she awaited her lover, and never awaited him in vain.

For some time all went well. Then one fateful night a storm smote the Hellespont. The waters of the strait were normally swift. But on this night, they rose like mountains crashing against each other as the wind drove them. At times the wind parted the ragged clouds and let a moment's moonlight through. In that brief illumination, Hero gauged the fury of the storm. She would not light the torch tonight. Still she did not return to the temple. Perhaps the storm would abate; Leander might yet come to her.

As the hours wore on, Hero's longing for him became too great to bear. She would place the torch, and somehow Leander would find his way to her. The gods had favored him thus far; they would not abandon him on this dangerous night. She hurried to light the flame.

Faithful to his love, Leander had been waiting as usual for Hero's signal. He did not expect to see it this night, but though the vigil was hopeless, he felt nearer to her as he peered through the storm.

Suddenly he saw a dart of light. He waited. It could be a trick of the imagination. No, there it was again and in the familiar place. Hero had set out the torch! That fact erased the threat of wind and tide. Eagerly he dived into the water and struck out for the opposite shore.

Before he had taken many strokes, Leander knew that he was doomed. Desperately he fought to stay above the waves, for he could make no progress through them. Once when he was lifted high he tried to see the torch, to know in which direction he should try to go. But there was no flame now. Wind and rain had extinguished it. He was in a wilderness of wind and water, with nothing to guide him, and he was tiring fast. His limbs were unresponsive to his will, and gradually sea water entered his lungs. He struggled more and more feebly. At last a wall of water came crashing down that he could not fight his way out of. In a moment he was drowned.

High in her lonely, storm-swept tower Hero waited with guilty anxiety. She hoped Leander had ignored her signal if, indeed, he had even seen it. A check shortly after she had placed the torch had told her it had gone out. Surely he had not seen it. More certainly he would not expect it on such a night as this. If only she had not placed that signal! How could she have been so selfish? So, accusing and hoping, Hero waited through the night.

At the first sign of dawn, she left the tower. The sea was calmer now. She descended the slippery stairs to the water's edge where rocks loomed in the feeble light. Hero approached the rocks, wading to her knees in the swirling surf. Suddenly she cried out. Floating between the rocks was the broken body of Leander. Hero stood for a long moment, gazing upon it in the slowly strengthening light. Shocked and despairing, she turned and started climbing the long stairway. When she reached the top of the tower, she paused to look out across the still turbulent waters through which Leander had come to her. She dropped her gaze to where his lifeless body now floated in the surf.

Then Hero flung herself from the tower to find death beside him.

For many centuries the factual aspects of this old tale were doubted. No man could swim the Hellespont at any point, it was affirmed. But a dashing English poet, Lord Byron, decided to test Leander's feat. While on a visit to Greece and Turkey, Lord Byron swam the Hellespont between Abydos and Sestos in May, 1810. Others have done it since.

PYRAMUS · AND · THISBE

8

PYRAMUS WAS A HANDSOME YOUTH and Thisbe as lovely as any maiden of the East. They lived as neighbors in Babylon, but their two houses were really one house separated by a common wall which ran straight through it.

Nearness is often a stimulant to romance, and since these two were so favored by nature, it was not surprising that they should fall in love. But their parents had other plans for them and looked with disfavor upon their romance. The two were forbidden to speak to each other, and though they met coming and going each day, the best they could hope for was to steal a sly glance or exchange a quick smile.

It may have been a fault in the construction of the wall that divided the two families, or it may just have been from the years of decay. Whatever may have caused it, a crack opened in the wall. It was not a wide opening; one could not have put a finger through it. But it was wide enough to convey the whispers of two lovers, and Pyramus and Thisbe were not slow to find it.

Each night, when both their houses were still, the pair would creep to the crack in the wall, Pyramus on his side, Thisbe on hers, and whisper sweet words to each other. Sometimes they would put their lips to the crack and feel each other's breath.

"Why do you thus tempt and thwart us, jealous wall?" Pyramus once said miserably. But he knew that if the crack were wider it would quickly be discovered. What they now had was better than anything they had had before. So, resigned, they kissed the wall when at last they said goodnight, wondering how much longer they could endure the sweet torment.

Finally they agreed to a desperate plan. They would steal separately from their homes when night blanketed the city and go beyond the walls to a well-known tomb. There no frustrating wall would be between them. Nor would there be anyone there to see them. A large tree grew beside the tomb, and they arranged that whoever came first to the trysting place would hide behind the tree.

The night agreed upon arrived, and Thisbe, a veil concealing her face, slipped as soundlessly as a shadow from her father's house. The moon was bright, and she kept close to the house walls as she hastened to the nearest city gate.

She reached the tomb safely, and finding Pyramus nowhere in sight, Thisbe sat down under the tree to wait. The tree was a mulberry, and its branches hung heavily loaded with snow-white fruit. Thisbe gazed happily about her, reveling in the beauty of this moonlit night and impatient for the arrival of her lover. Suddenly she tensed. Then she leaped to her feet with a cry of alarm.

At a little distance beyond the tree, a lioness had walked out of some bushes. She had made a kill and, her jaws bloody from her recent feasting, she was coming to drink from a spring nearby.

The frightened Thisbe darted away from the tree toward a cave behind it. She ran with such speed that her veil went streaming behind her and fell to the ground in the very path of the lioness. Just as Thisbe gained the safety of the cave, the lioness came upon the veil. She took it into her bloodied jaws, played with it a moment, and then dropped it, ragged and bloody. She then sauntered quietly to the spring, drank her fill, and trotted off.

A few moments later Pyramus reached the scene. He looked eagerly toward the tree. There was no sign of Thisbe. Pyramus advanced toward the trysting place. Suddenly he halted, staring at the moonlit ground. Unmistakably imprinted, there were a lion's tracks. He glanced, horrified, to where Thisbe should be waiting under the tree. It was then he beheld her veil on the ground. He rushed toward it, picked it up, and looked at the blood. He saw how the veil was torn, and he guessed at once what had happened to his beloved Thisbe.

"It is I who have caused your death," he mourned. "It was I who proposed this meeting and urged it on you. But you shall not die alone, my dear one. On this night two lovers will pay the price of their love. Let the lion return; let it tear me limb for limb. I have no wish to live without my Thisbe."

But the lioness did not return, and the sorrowing youth, with the veil in his hands, moved toward the tree where Thisbe should have been waiting. For a moment he buried his face in the veil; then he drew the sword at his side and plunged it into himself. As the blood gushed forth upon the ground and sank into the roots of the tree, its white fruit slowly turned to a dark, almost purple, red.

Thisbe had waited a long time in the cave and her fears had somewhat diminished. She came cautiously toward the cave mouth and looked out to see if the lioness had gone. All seemed well, and she started toward the tree—which for some reason looked strange to her. Then she saw the body on the ground and ran toward it.

"Pyramus, oh Pyramus, what dreadful thing is this?" she cried as she threw herself down beside him. She saw the veil still crushed in his hand. She saw the sword dripping blood, and she saw the closed face of her lover. As the awful truth was suddenly known to her, she had no wish to live.

"A wall separated us in life, but death shall not separate us now," she said, reaching for the sword. She rose and placed its point beneath her breast. In the next second, Thisbe, pierced to the heart, lay quiet beside Pyramus.

With the dawn, the tragedy was known and its cause understood. The lion's tracks, the bloody veil, and the crimson sword told the tale all too plainly. The parents of both houses mourned their losses and blamed themselves. They tried to compensate for their harsh blindness by having the ashes of the two lovers placed in a single urn. So at last Pyramus and Thisbe were united. And forever after the mulberry tree has borne magenta fruit.

DEMETER

THE · GOOD · GODDESS

BEFORE HE HAD LEARNED of seed time and harvest, man wandered the earth in search of animals to supply him with food. As the great herds moved, man moved with them, so that he never had a fixed home place and was ever at the mercy of wind and weather.

Then came the Good Goddess, Demeter, one of the first Olympians and a sister of Zeus. Prometheus had given fire to man; now Demeter would show mortals how to plow the soil and how to plant seeds and reap their harvest. Men stopped their wandering and lived surrounded by their fields of grain, the gift of Demeter. Thus civilization began to develop. Men built houses; they accumulated household possessions; they domesticated animals to serve them. Most important of all, they were able to store their corn and barley to have throughout the year, enough even to carry them over a bad harvest.

All this they owed to Demeter, the Corn-Goddess. They believed that she was present on every threshing floor to separate the wheat from the chaff at harvest time. Her most important festival was held then.

She was a beautiful goddess, this queen of heaven. Her hair was the color of ripe grain and out of her face shone the beauty of contentment and fulfillment. Her slender body moved with dignity upon the earth, and wherever she went she was beloved and revered by everyone.

Persephone

DEMETER HAD A DAUGHTER named Persephone. Unlike the other Olympians, who for the most part took a casual view of their parenthood, Demeter loved her daughter with all the warmth and devotion of a human mother.

Persephone was a daughter easy to love. Besides her beauty, she had a disposition as sunny and bright as the springtime. Wherever she went there seemed to be a flowering all about her. The sun seemed brighter; the birds sang more prettily. All nature seemed to welcome this lightly stepping daughter of the fertility goddess, Demeter.

One who had noticed her charms was Hades, king of the Underworld. He spoke to his brother Zeus of his de-

sire to have Persephone for his queen, and Zeus agreed
to arrange it for him.

In the springtime of that year, Persephone and her
friends were out in the fields gathering wild flowers.
Violets, cyclamen, and red poppies carpeted the ground
in brilliant colors, and the girls went gaily about their
pleasant task of filling baskets with the bright blooms.

On the edge of the field where it joined a shadowy
grove, Persephone suddenly saw a blossom such as she
had never seen before. It stood well above the ground
and was of such beauty that she stood amazed before it.
Some say it was the asphodel, the spiky plant that still
sends forth its blooms in April.

As Persephone reached to pluck it, the ground quickly
opened beside her, and out shot the golden chariot of
Hades, drawn by two black horses. Holding the reins in
one hand, the god seized Persephone with the other and
swung her into the chariot. The basket fell from her
hands, spilling the blossoms in a bright flood, and she
cried out for her mother. Again and again she cried, but
the chariot never slackened its speed. Hades called to the
horses, and they put forth their best effort, hurtling
through lakes and across streams. They came at last to a
wide pool where Arethusa, a nymph, rose from the water
and, spreading her arms wide, sought to stop the chariot.

"Let the maiden go," the nymph cried. "Demeter is
my friend, and you shall not abduct her daughter."

Arethusa had not always been a water nymph. Once
she had been a hunter and a follower of Artemis. But one

unlucky day, while she was bathing in a clear pool, the river Alpheus saw her and fell in love with her. And though the maiden ran from his advances, still, of course, a river could continue running forever, and there was no way Arethusa could escape Alpheus. She called on Artemis to save her. The goddess answered her prayer by changing her into the fountain that now stood in the way of Hades' chariot.

But the king of the Underworld seized his scepter and struck the water with it. Instantly a cavern opened before him, and he drove the team into it. Thus did Persephone come to the dark regions of the Dead.

Demeter had heard her daughter's frantic cries and at once had begun a search for her. She was nowhere to be found. For nine days the Corn-Goddess searched throughout the world, seeking Persephone and grieving for her loss.

At night she lighted torches and wandered under the stars; during the day she continued her weary tramping under the heat of the sun. Caught up in her own sorrow, she was indifferent to the needs of field and grove. Earth began to suffer from her neglect.

One day, weary and almost spent, she saw a small cottage. It had a thatched roof and a small door and looked humble in the extreme. But the goddess was tormented by thirst and approached it for a drink of water. The good housewife, not recognizing Demeter in the disguise she had assumed of an old woman, bade her enter, and fixed her a drink which she sweetened with barley. The goddess in her grief had denied herself all refreshment. She took the cup and drank from it greedily.

A son of the housewife stood nearby, watching Demeter, an ugly sneer on his face. At last he burst into rude laughter at the old woman as she gulped the drink down. Demeter lifted her lips from the cup and looked at the boy with angry eyes. Then, before he knew what was happening, she flung the remains of the drink full in his face. A strange thing happened. The boy began to shrink. His legs and arms shortened, and he started to grow a tail. In a moment he had become a newt, with marks on his body duplicating the barley seeds that had been in the cup. His mother, greatly wondering, put out her hands and tried to seize him, but he evaded her and crawled away between two stones, a harmless creature.

Demeter's wanderings at last brought her to the fountain Arethusa. Here she saw floating on its surface a bright scarf that she recognized at once as Persephone's. She wept to see it, and the sounds of her mourning brought the nymph up from the waters.

"Be comforted, O mother of the lost Persephone. I have seen your daughter. I saw her a captive of Hades when his chariot dived beneath this fountain. And roaming the dark regions under these waters, I have seen Persephone throned as his queen. This is her fate, to rule the Underworld, the region of the Dead, with him."

Demeter stood as one turned to stone. These were terrible words that fell upon her ears. Her daughter, her dear laughter-loving, springtime girl confined in that dread place! Never to see sunlight; never to see fields or flowers; never to know her mother's love again. Only the ghosts of the Dead for company! It was more than even a goddess could endure. She raved as she stood there and cursed the earth. Demeter's horror was entirely justified. The Underworld was a dreadful place, and Persephone had suffered a most unhappy fate.

The entrance to this abode of the Dead lay somewhere to the west, beyond the River of Ocean. All manner of griefs haunted that entrance: Anxiety, Disease, Old Age, and War among them. Past the entrance a gloomy passage led down to where several rivers fanned out, barring the way. Across one of these, the river Styx, the old boatman Charon poled his ferry, carrying the souls on whose dead lips someone had remembered to place a coin to pay Charon's ferry fee.

All manner of dead lined the riverbanks awaiting the crossing. Old and young, beggars and princes—they waited their turns as the glum old ferryman with his white beard and filthy cloak slowly poled the boat toward them. Some he refused to take. These were the souls of the unburied dead. They were doomed to remain clamoring on the far shore of Hades forever, denied alike the torments of Tartarus and the fair Elysian Fields.

Once across the Styx, the Dead were treated to the sight of Cerberus. Chained to his kennel, Cerberus prevented from entering any who might have circumvented old Charon.

Deeper into the Underworld lay Limbo, a region given over to famed warriors. Most dreadful and deepest of all lay Tartarus, the region of the damned. One of these was Ixion, who had dared to insult Hera, wife of Zeus. The All-father had punished Ixion by having him chained to a perpetually revolving flaming wheel. Tantalus was another whom Zeus had sentenced to eternal punishment. He had served up his own son, Pelops, as a feast to the gods. Eventually, Pelops was restored to life, but one of his shoulders was ivory. Demeter had unwittingly eaten part of it during the grim feast. Now Tantalus stood in a pool of water tormented by unending thirst. The pool reached to his lips, but whenever Tantalus bent his head to drink, the water receded from him. Over his head hung luscious ripe fruit, but when he reached for it, the branch snapped up and away from his hand.

Still another doomed soul was Sisyphus, a king of Corinth. His punishment for betraying Zeus was to push a huge stone up a hill. Whenever he neared the top with his task almost complete, the stone slipped from his grasp and went rolling to the bottom. Indeed, Tartarus was Hades at its worst.

The best part of the gloomy Underworld was the Elysian Fields, or Elysium, where the departed souls of good mortals lived in perpetual bliss. It had a sun and stars of its own, playing fields and leafy groves. Here lived the souls destined to be born again, though, having drunk the waters of the river Lethe, they would remember nothing of their past.

Besides Hades himself, there was one other Immortal who was important to the Underworld. This was a Titan named Hecate. Zeus had spared her because she was a goddess of fertility, almost as important to crops and herds as Demeter. But as time went by, Hecate became a goddess of the night and of crossroads and was closely associated with Hades and the Underworld. Sorceresses invoked her, and she haunted crossroads at night. No traveler ever lingered in such places after dark for fear of Hecate and her hellhounds. To ward off her curse, people often left food offerings, Hecate's suppers, where two roads crossed.

It was over this dreary kingdom and its sad inhabitants that Persephone had become queen. Where once she had been light-hearted and playful, she now sat through the long dark hours grieving for her mother and the upper world of sun and flowers, where Demeter also grieved most terribly and punished Earth with her sorrow.

Eleusis

THE EARTH BECAME barren. Fields were fallow. Cattle sickened and died. Famine threatened all the land. But Demeter continued to be indifferent to the sufferings of

Earth. She cared for nothing but the return of her daughter and trudged the roads in aimless seeking.

At last, still in her disguise of an old woman, she came to the city of Eleusis. Here she approached a well where the daughters of the king came to fill their water jars. The day was hot. Demeter sat down on the well's brink to rest herself. She drew her dusty skirts about her and let her shoulders sag. It was not long before the young princesses found her. She looked so old and so weary, they felt pity for her.

"Poor old woman"—one of them addressed her—"you look as if you had come a long way. You must be tired."

Demeter lifted up the dark length of cloth that had been shading her head from the sun and looked at the circle of cheerful young faces.

"The day has been too much for you," said another. "Demeter is punishing the earth. The sun burns fiercely day after day! The fields are drying up; even this well is lowering."

"Who are you and where do you come from?" asked a third.

Demeter sighed and answered like one for whom speaking was a chore. "My name is Dois and I come from Crete."

The princesses looked at one another.

"How sad she sounds," whispered the first one who had spoken. The others nodded. Withdrawing a bit, they

held a private counsel. Then they approached the old woman.

"We are the daughters of Celeus, king of this country. Our mother is Metaneira, and she is kind," said the eldest princess. "Let us take you to her, and she will give you refuge."

The weary, grief-stricken goddess found such kindness irresistible. When the girls had filled their water jars, she followed them to the palace.

Queen Metaneira received the stranger as kindly as had her daughters.

"When you have refreshed yourself," she told the old woman, "you may take over the care of my infant son, Demophoön. For as long as you tend him faithfully, you will have a home with us."

The princesses were not only kind, but gay. One of them was a prankster and a tease. It was not long before Demeter was smiling occasionally at her antics. And there could be no doubt of the new nurse's affection for her young charge. She cared for the baby tenderly. But this was no ordinary nurse!

Each day, Demeter annointed Demophoön with ambrosia, the food of the gods. And at night when all within the palace slept, she laid him in the heart of a sacred fire. This was to burn away all that was mortal in the tiny body and at last render it immortal and one with the gods. Thus did Demeter plan to reward the family who had been so kind to her.

But one night Metaneira woke and was overcome with a deep compulsion to visit the nursery. What was her horror to discover her baby surrounded by flames and his nursemaid standing quietly by, making no move to save him! Metaneira let out a terrible scream. Demeter snatched the child from the fire and laid him none too gently on the floor. Gone now was the old woman. In her place stood a radiant goddess. The whole room was filled with the brightness of her heavenly figure.

"Poor foolish woman," the goddess scolded her. "Could you not have stayed your curiosity for one more night? Why did you come spying now? Have you not seen that your baby was thriving and happy? Have I not tended him faithfully each day? Had you but waited one more night, he would have been immortal."

"Do not be angry," begged Metaneira. "How could I know that one of the Immortals served my child? Only tell me what we must do to appease you."

"You must raise a temple in my honor here in Eleusis." Demeter told her. "Its rites will be secret, and the fame of the Mysteries of Eleusis will spread throughout all the world. I will take up my abode in that temple far from Olympus, and there I shall stay until my dear Persephone is returned to me."

Work on the temple began the very next day and never stopped until it was finished. Faithful to her promise, Demeter returned to Eleusis and made it her abode.

Persephone's Fate

WHEN ZEUS CONNIVED with his brother Hades in the abduction of Persephone, he had not reckoned on the depth of Demeter's grief and outrage. The Father of Gods, all but indifferent to his own offspring, had failed to realize the deep devotion the Corn-Goddess lavished upon her daughter. Her mourning for the loss of her child was great enough to make Demeter forget her duties to Earth. And so Earth suffered.

At last it became clear to Zeus that the girl would have to be returned, and he ordered Hades to take her to the temple in Eleusis where Demeter awaited her.

But Hades was not to be deprived of his queen so easily.

It was well understood by gods and men alike that no one could ever return from the Underworld who had taken nourishment there. In all the time Persephone had been captive in that dark realm no food or drink had passed her lips. So the wily Hades saw a possible way to keep his love. He would get the better of Zeus!

On the edge of the Elysian Fields there grew a small tree with bright green and somewhat feathery foliage. Its fruit was about the size of an apple, and when it ripened and split, its interior was shown to be filled with blood-red seeds that were full of delicious juice. It was called a pomegranate.

Hardly had Zeus issued his command that Persephone

be freed, than Hades visited the pomegranate tree. Carefully he surveyed its branches. Then he plucked the largest and most luscious of its fruit. One side was split, revealing plump red seeds, sweet and juicy. Smiling to himself, he carried it to the dim hall where Persephone sat.

She did not raise her eyes as Hades approached her, but kept her chin in her hand and her gaze on the stone floor.

He came close to the throne and held out the pomegranate. "Here, Persephone, is something to comfort you. In all the long time you have been here neither food nor drink has passed your lips. Here is something to refresh you."

Wearily Persephone raised her head and regarded him. Then she glanced at the fruit shining in his hand. For a long moment she considered it; she was strongly tempted, for her need was great. At last she reached for it. Then, almost idly, she plucked out a seed and put it into her mouth. Its fresh sweetness exploded upon her tongue and she ate another. And another. And another.

When she had swallowed the juice and the pulp of the fourth seed, she looked up suddenly and saw Hades' eyes devouring her with a look so avid and triumphant that it startled her. The pomegranate fell from her hand, and a nameless foreboding settled upon her.

Shortly after, Hermes appeared to escort Persephone back to the upper world. Zeus had ordered that she be returned to her mother.

Persephone sprang from her throne at the glad announcement, her foreboding forgotten. She was to leave this odious place and this odious king; she would see her mother again! She did not try to conceal her impatience to start while the black horses were being harnessed to the golden chariot. When all was ready, Persephone and Hermes mounted into the chariot. Hermes spoke to the horses, and they dashed away along the dim corridors of the Underworld until they burst from the gates of Hades into the world of sunlight.

Swiftly the horses carried them across the wide plain to the city of Eleusis, where Demeter awaited her daughter. Straight to the temple Hermes guided the team. They had hardly skidded to a halt when Persephone sprang from the chariot and into her mother's arms. The good citizens of Eleusis were moved to tears as they witnessed the happy reunion of this goddess mother and daughter.

For a time Demeter and Persephone could talk of nothing but the long sad year of their separation.

Suddenly Demeter said, "You ate nothing during the time Hades kept you captive, did you?"

Persephone looked worried. "Nothing, really," she said. "On the last day Hades brought me a pomegranate and I ate four of its seeds."

Demeter gave a terrible cry. It shook the temple confines and brought its priestesses running.

"Did you not know," the anguished mother demanded, "that whoever eats *anything at all* in that accursed place may never depart from it again?"

Now it was Persephone's turn to send up a wail to heaven. Such howls of grief issued from the temple that Olympus was alerted and Zeus sent to ask what the reason for this fresh outburst could be.

When he learned the truth, Zeus sought a compromise with Hades.

"It is true you tricked us," he told his brother. "But we cannot risk Demeter's further punishment of Earth. You may not keep Persephone permanently within your realm. Tell me, how many pomegranate seeds did she eat?"

"Four," replied Hades, and his voice was surly.

"Then," said Zeus, "she shall be your queen for four months of each year. For the rest of the time she will be with her mother on Earth."

So it was that Persephone went again to the Underworld. And during the four months that she reigned there each year as Hades' queen, the earth was bare of fruit and blossom. The sun rarely shone, and rain like Demeter's own tears showered down upon the barren soil. All nature mourned with Demeter the loss of Persephone.

But when at last the four months were ended and Persephone again came forth from her dreary kingdom, all Earth smiled. Buds opened on the trees, the hills put on a mantle of green, and the fields were bright with flowers.

Demeter, too, had to be satisfied with this settlement of the quarrel between her and Hades. At least she would have her dear Persephone with her most of the time. As if to compensate Earth for the punishment she had made it suffer, Demeter now made the soil more fertile than it ever had been.

The vines hung with rich clusters of grapes and the wheat bent full-headed on its stalks. Cattle and sheep and goats were fat and glossy, and there was no disease among them. Men smiled as they went about their tasks, happy in the work that this abundance brought them.

Demeter did more. She called upon the princes of Eleusis, the very ones who had built her temple. She selected one, Triptolemus, the brother of the infant Demophoön, and gave him a chariot drawn by dragons with wings.

"You shall be my representative upon the earth, Triptolemus," the goddess told him. "Your mission is to take seed grain and go throughout the world telling men how to till the soil and plant the seeds and harvest the grain when it is ripe."

The young prince gladly consented to serve the Good Goddess, whose suffering and generous bounty combined to make her the most revered of all the queens of heaven.

Glossary

Achilles	a kĭl′ēz	Calydon	kăl′i don
Adonis	a dŏn′ĭs	Calydonian	kăl′ĭ dō′nĭ an
Aeneas	a nē′as	Castor	kas′ter
Aglaia	a glā′ya	Celeus	sē′li us
Alpheus	ăl fē′us	Cerberus	ser′ber us
Althaea	al thē′a	Charon	kā′rŏn
Anchises	ăn kī′sēz	Cupid	kū′pĭd
Aphrodite	ăf rŏ dī′tē	Cyprian	sĭp′rĭ an
Apollo	a pŏl′ō		
Arcadia	ar kā′dĭ a	Dardania	dar dā′ni a
Ares	ā′rēs	Demeter	de mē′ter
Arethusa	ăr e thū′za	Dionysus	dī ō nī′sŭs
Argonauts	ar′gō nawts	Dois	dō′is
Artemis	ar′tĕ mĭs	Demophoön	dē mŏf′ō ōn
Atalanta	ăt′a lăn′ta		
Athena	a thē′na	Elysian	ē lĭz′ĭ ăn
		Elysium	ē lĭz′Ĭ ŭm
Cadmus	kăd′mŭs	Eros	ē′rŏs

Euphrosyne	u frŏs'ĭ nē	Oeneus	ē'nūs
		Olympus	ō lĭm'pŭs
Galatea	găl'a tē'a		
		Peleus	pē'lūs
Hadez	hā'dēz	Pelops	pē'lŏps
Harmonia	har mō'ni a	Persephone	per sĕf'ō nē
Harpies	har'pĭz	Phrygia	frĭj'ĭ a
Hecate	hĕk'a tē	Pluto	plōō'tō
Hephaestus	hē fĕs'tŭs	Pollux	pŏl'ŭks
Hera	hē'ra	Prometheus	prō mē'thŭs
Hero	hĕr'ō	Psyche	sī'kē
Hermes	hŭr'mēz	Pygmalion	pĭg mā'lĭ ŏn
Hippomenes	hĭ pŏm'e nēz	Pyramus	pĭr'a mŭs
Ida	ī'da	Sisyphus	sĭs'ĭ fŭs
Ixion	ĭks ī'ŏn	Styx	stĭks
Jason	jā'sŭn	Tantalus	tăn'ta lŭs
		Tartarus	tar'tăr us
Leander	le ăn'der	Thalia	tha lī'a
Limbo	lim'bō	Thebes	thēbz
		Theseus	thē'sŭs
		Thisbe	thĭz'bē
Medea	me dē'a	Triptolemus	trĭp tŏl'e·mŭs
Meleager	mĕl'e ā'jer	Trojan	trō'jan
Metaneira	mĕt ă nī'ra	Troy	troi
Minotaur	mĭn'ō tawr		
		Zephyr	zĕf'er
Nestor	nĕs'tawr	Zeus	zūs

ABOUT THE AUTHOR

DORIS GATES was born and grew up in California, not far from Carmel, where she now makes her home. She was for many years head of the Children's Department of the Fresno County Free Library in Fresno, California. Their new children's room, which was dedicated in 1969, is called the Doris Gates Room in her honor. It was at this library that she became well known as a storyteller, an activity she has continued through the years. The Greek myths— the fabulous tales of gods and heroes, of bravery and honor, of meanness and revenge—have always been among her favorite stories to tell.

After the publication of several of her books, Doris Gates gave up her library career to devote full time to writing books for children. Her many well-known books include *A Morgan for Melinda* and the Newbery Honor Book, *Blue Willow*.